Chopsticks

JESSICA ANTHONY

RODRIGO CORRAL

RAZORBILL
AN IMPRINT OF
PENGUIN GROUP (USA) INC.

Chopsticks

RAZORBILL

Published by the Penguin Group
Penguin Young Readers Group
345 Hudson Street, New York, New York 10014, U.S.A.
Penguin Group (USA) Inc., 375 Hudson Street, New York, New York 10014, U.S.A.
Penguin Group (Canada), 90 Eglinton Avenue East, Suite 700, Toronto, Ontario, Canada M4P 2Y3 (a division of Pearson Penguin Canada Inc.)
Penguin Books Ltd, 80 Strand, London WC2R ORL, England
Penguin Ireland, 25 St Stephen's Green, Dublin 2, Ireland (a division of Penguin Books Ltd)
Penguin Group (Australia), 250 Camberwell Road, Camberwell, Victoria 3124, Australia (a division of Pearson Australia Group Pty Ltd)
Penguin Books India Pvt Ltd, 11 Community Centre, Panchsheel Park, New Delhi - 110 017, India
Penguin Group (NZ), 67 Apollo Drive, Mairangi Bay, Auckland 1311, New Zealand (a division of Pearson New Zealand Ltd)
Penguin Books (South Africa) (Pty) Ltd, 24 Sturdee Avenue, Rosebank, Johannesburg 2196, South Africa

Penguin Books Ltd, Registered Offices: 80 Strand, London WC2R ORL, England

10 9 8 7 6 5 4 3 2 1

Copyright © 2012 Jessica Anthony and Rodrigo Corral
All rights reserved

ISBN 978-1-59514-435-5

Library of Congress Cataloging-in-Publication Data is available

Printed in China

For my parents, who sent me off into the world, and for Jon, who brings me home. —Jessica

For Tea Why, Ty. —Rodrigo

Breaking
News
4
New York

BREAKING NEWS

FOX
NEWS
LIVE

//FOX

COPS TRYING TO GET ACCESS TO

"And now, breaking news out of the Bronx. World famous pianist Glory Fleming is missing. She was last seen wearing a blue Sergio "The Marvel" Martinez boxing robe,

BREAKING NEWS

◉**2 GLORY FLEMING, WORLD FAMOU**

and currently resides **on** Usher Avenue with her father, Victor Fleming. Her mother, now deceased, was a wine distributor for W.J. Import-Export..."

Ouverturen-Album. für Pianoforte zu vier Händen arrangiert, Hugo Ulrich - 1896 Peters, Leipzig

CHAPTER 1

Renowned Piano Prodigy Disappears

By Helen Mundt

Two days ago, the famous concert pianist Gloria "Glory" Fleming disappeared from Golden Hands Rest Facility, an institution for musical prodigies here in the Bronx.

Praised by critics as "The Brecht of the Piano," Ms. Fleming is known for her modern innovations on classical repertoire. The young pianist received rave reviews until six months ago, when exhaustion caused an infamous performance at Carnegie Hall. Fellow patients at Golden Hands recall the seventeen-year-old regularly playing the whimsical children's waltz "Chopsticks," an obsession which worsened during her tenure at Golden Hands.

The evening she went missing, Gloria Fleming had apparently played the waltz for over seven hours.

Ms. Fleming was raised in the large Victorian house at 121 Usher Avenue with her father and piano instructor, Victor Fleming, where he still resides. Her mother, Maria Torres Fleming, a wine expert who worked for the South American wine distributor W.J. Import-Export,

died in a motorcycle accident in 2000.

Glory Fleming was last seen walking the corridor from a practice room to her personal quarters. She was wearing drawstring pajamas and a blue silk boxing robe with the name of the famous Argentine boxer SERGIO "THE MARVEL" MARTINEZ embroidered in white on the back. However these items were found yesterday morning on the lawn outside Golden Hands.

Please contact this paper or the police as soon as possible with any information regarding her whereabouts.

Bronx Traffic Cop Assaulted

By Justin Roschenber

BRONX TIMES REPORTER   MONDAY, DECEMBER 7, 2009   WWW.BXTIMES.COM

broke down resulting in a hold- ... tion, the manager called up the ... to send a towing ...

18 Months
Earlier

"Because
our love
is _wild_."
—V

To the victor goes the spoils.
City Hall, 1990

Marriage Certificate

STATE OF NEW YORK

FORM 27

THE VITAL STATISTIC ACT

MA 3909

NAME OF BRIDEGROOM	FLEMING, VICTOR
PLACE OF BIRTH	NEW YORK, NY
NAME OF BRIDE	TORRES, MARIA
PLACE OF BIRTH	NEW YORK, NY
DATE OF MARRIAGE	OCTOBER 16TH, 1990
PLACE OF MARRIAGE	NEW YORK CITY HALL
DATE OF REGISTRATION	OCTOBER 16TH, 1990

REGISTRATION NUMBER 1950-356

(REGISTRAR-GENERAL)

56922 TH

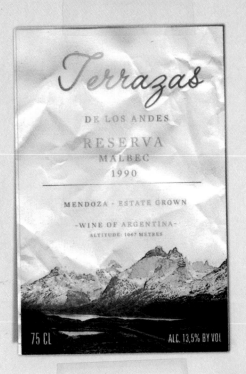

Terrazas

DE LOS ANDES

RESERVA
MALBEC
1990

MENDOZA · ESTATE GROWN

-WINE OF ARGENTINA-
ALTITUDE: 1067 METRES

75 CL   ALC. 13,5% BY VOL

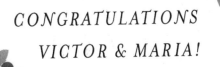

CONGRATULATIONS
VICTOR & MARIA!

FROM ALL OF US AT
W.J. IMPORT-EXPORT

W.J. Import-Export
Bringing the Wines of South America to You

Our Glory.

Glory's 7th birthday, 1999.
"The most beautiful cake in the
world, Mom." V was miffed.
He made the rose.

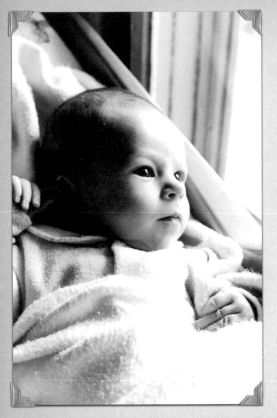

Darling Glory, 1992.

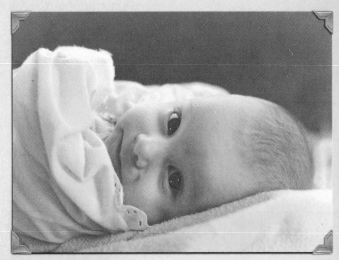

Oct. 20, 1999
Students of Victor Fleming

Afternoon Fall Recital
2 p.m.

Coney Island Museum

Introduced by Victor Fleming

Please join us for refreshments
following the performances.

n"

er"

on"

Gloria Fleming..**"Chopsticks Waltz"**
Arthur de Lulli (Euphemia
Allen)

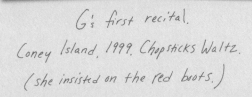

G's first recital.
Coney Island, 1999. Chopsticks Waltz.
(she insisted on the red boots.)

MERRY
CHRISTMAS

1999

May
this year
bring you joy!

Victor, Maria
and Glory

MERRY
CHRISTMAS
2000

Thank you for your
support during this
difficult year.
Best wishes for a safe
holiday season.

Victor & Glory

Monday, June 26, 2006

National Symphony Orchestra

The Kennedy Center

8 p.m.

Gloria Fleming

Piano Concerto No. 5 in E-flat Major, op. 73

Ludwig van Beethoven

THE NEW YORKER

JUNE 27. 2007

GOINGS ON ABOUT TOWN

CLASSICAL MUSIC

Russian Roulette
CARNEGIE HALL
881 7th Ave. (212) 287-7800. July 4. Gloria "Glory" Fleming, once a young piano prodigy from the Bronx, is now being heralded as "The Brecht of the Piano." She returns to New York for one night only in what promises to be a breakthrough performance of Prokofiev's "Obsession Diabolique." Other pieces from early twentieth-century Russian composers Mosolov and Krein to be showcased as well. (See page 32).

June 29-July 5, 2007

Wednesday 4
Classical

Piano prodigy **Gloria "Glory" Fleming** to play a tribute to Russian composers Mosolov, Krein and Prokofiev. The fifteen-year-old is known in many circles as "The Brecht of the Piano" for her innovative performances of classical pieces alongside modern scores. Her last performance at the Kennedy Center threaded motifs of major works by Bach and Beethoven with samples from the likes of Madonna, Frank Sinatra and The Beatles. Not to be missed.

One Night in Moscow

GLORIA
FLEMING

"The Brecht of the Piano"

Carnegie Hall-New York's favorite young pianist Gloria Fleming
will perform Prokofiev's "Obsession Diabolique" and other selections.
Limited seating available. For tickets, contact www.ticketmaster.com.

July 4ᵗʰ, 2007

July 4, 2007

CARNEGIE HALL

New York City
8 PM

The People's Concerts

GLORIA FLEMING
PIANO

Part One

Piano Sonata No. 2
in B minor, op. 4
Alexander Mosolov

Piano Sonata op. 34
Alexander Krein

Part Two

"Obsession Diabolique"
op.4, no. 4
Sergei Prokofiev

Local Piano Star Shines

By Helen Mundt

Blending early twentieth century Russian composers with modern rock music, last night fifteen-year-old Gloria Fleming performed a sophisticated repertoire to a riveted audience at Carnegie Hall.

In Part One of the program, Ms. Fleming peppered little-known Russian composer Alexander Mosolov's Piano Sonata No. 2 with motifs of the contemporary rock bands Pavement, Wilco and others.

But it was in Part Two where her talents truly shone.

To begin, Ms. Fleming launched into Prokofiev's "Obsession Diabolique" with the unwavering roar of a master. Slowly, as the momentum built, she offered her audience a taste of the dissonant notes F and G, the opening chord to the children's waltz "Chopsticks."

What followed was a breathtaking collage of simplicity and extravagance unlike anything this reporter has ever heard.

In Ms. Fleming's hands, the notes accumulated like numbers destined for some impossible mathematical formula—perhaps the unknowable theorum of the human heart?—leaving us only to wonder where she can possibly go from here.

Victor Fleming is planning a national tour for his daughter this fall.

New Public Pool Opening

By Colleen Boothby

In an era of private grand New York City ha for the publi

WWW.BXTIMES.COM THURSDAY , JULY 5, 2007 BRONX TIMES REPORTER

Rich Valley Farm Goat Milk Soap

Chapter Two

6-8am Schulmann, Chopin
8-9am Breakfast
9-11am Bartok
11am-noon German
12pm-1pm Lunch
1-3pm Algebra, Spanish
3-4pm Outside Hour
4-5pm Tchaikowsky
5-6pm Dinner
6-8pm Stravinsky, Shostakovich
8-9pm Free Hour
9pm Bed

"Gloria, did you hear me? Turn off that television and go to bed."

"And now, ladies and gentlemen, here is a great performer: Jo Ann Castle. Jo Ann has had a favorite song since she was a little girl."

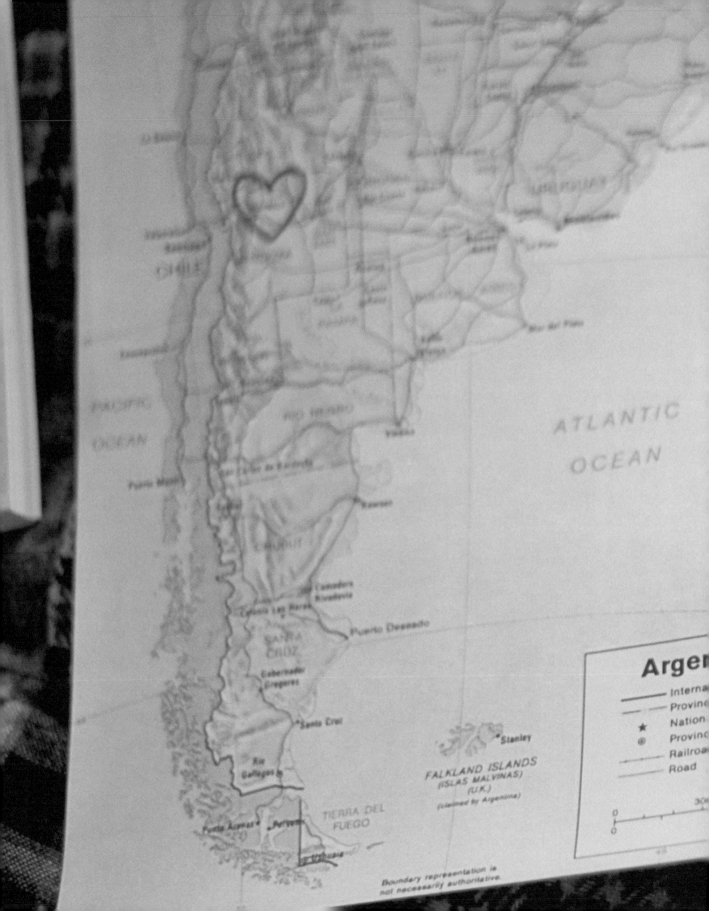

"Listen to your mother, *Hijo!*"

1500 Waters Place
Bronx NY 10461

WD

FRANCISCO MENDOZA

SOPHOMORE

WILLARD DUNN SCHOOL FOR BOYS
1500 Waters Place · Bronx, NY 10461 · (718) 862-3004 · fax: (718) 862-9987

LOCKER 451

COMBINATION

26-45-26

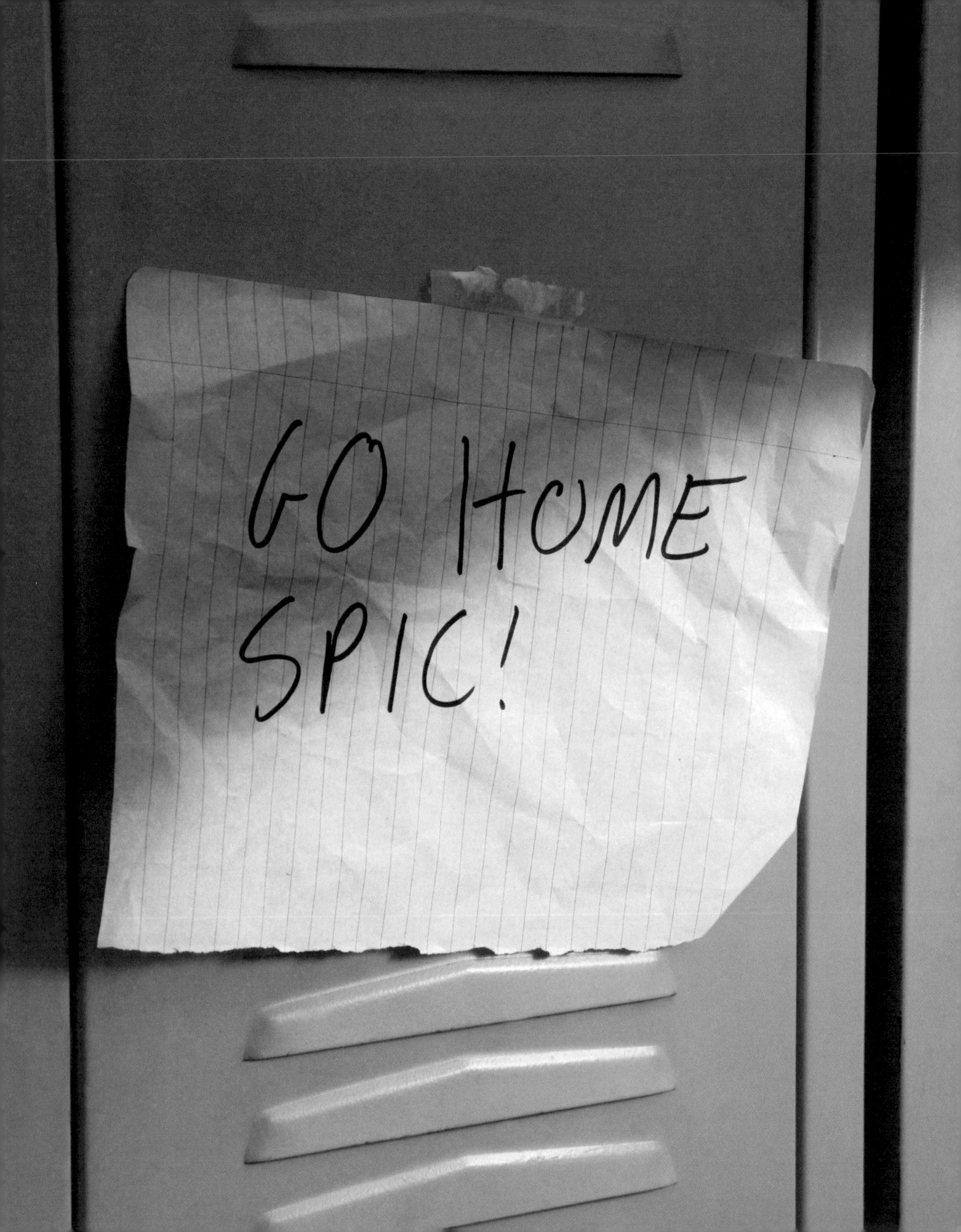
GO HOME
SPIC!

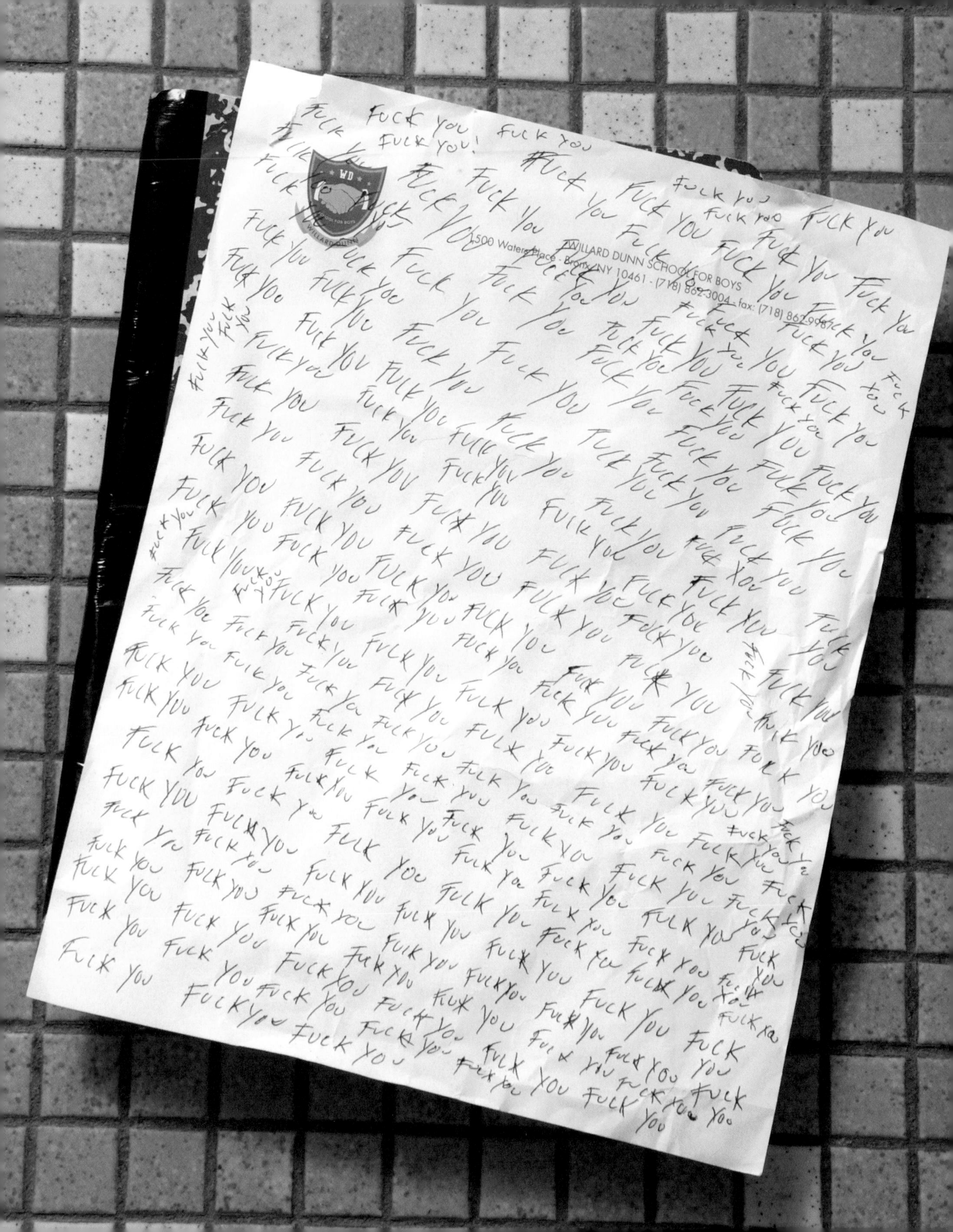
WD
WILLARD DUNN
WILLARD DUNN SCHOOL FOR BOYS
1500 Waters Place · Bronx, NY 10461 · (718) 862-3004 · fax: (718) 862-998
FUCK YOU

Happy Birthday, Mi Dulce.
Sixteen years ago, you
came into our lives! A
bottle of wine from that
year, and a little something
else too. We love you.

HAPPY BIRTHDAY,
HIJO.
-YOUR PAPA

SOCIETÉ CIVILE DU DOMAINE DE LA ROMANÉE-CONTI

PROPRIÉTAIRE A VOSNE-ROMANÉE (CÔTE D'OR)

ROMANÉE-CONTI

APPELLATION ROMANÉE-CONTI CONTROLÉE

5.124 Bouteilles Recoltées

N. 000291

L'ASSOCIÉ GÉRANT

ANNÉE 1991

Mise en bouteille au domaine

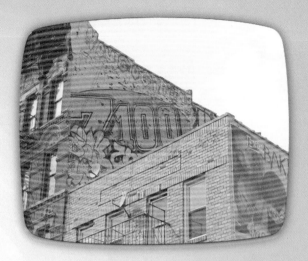

Come over
if you want...
-G

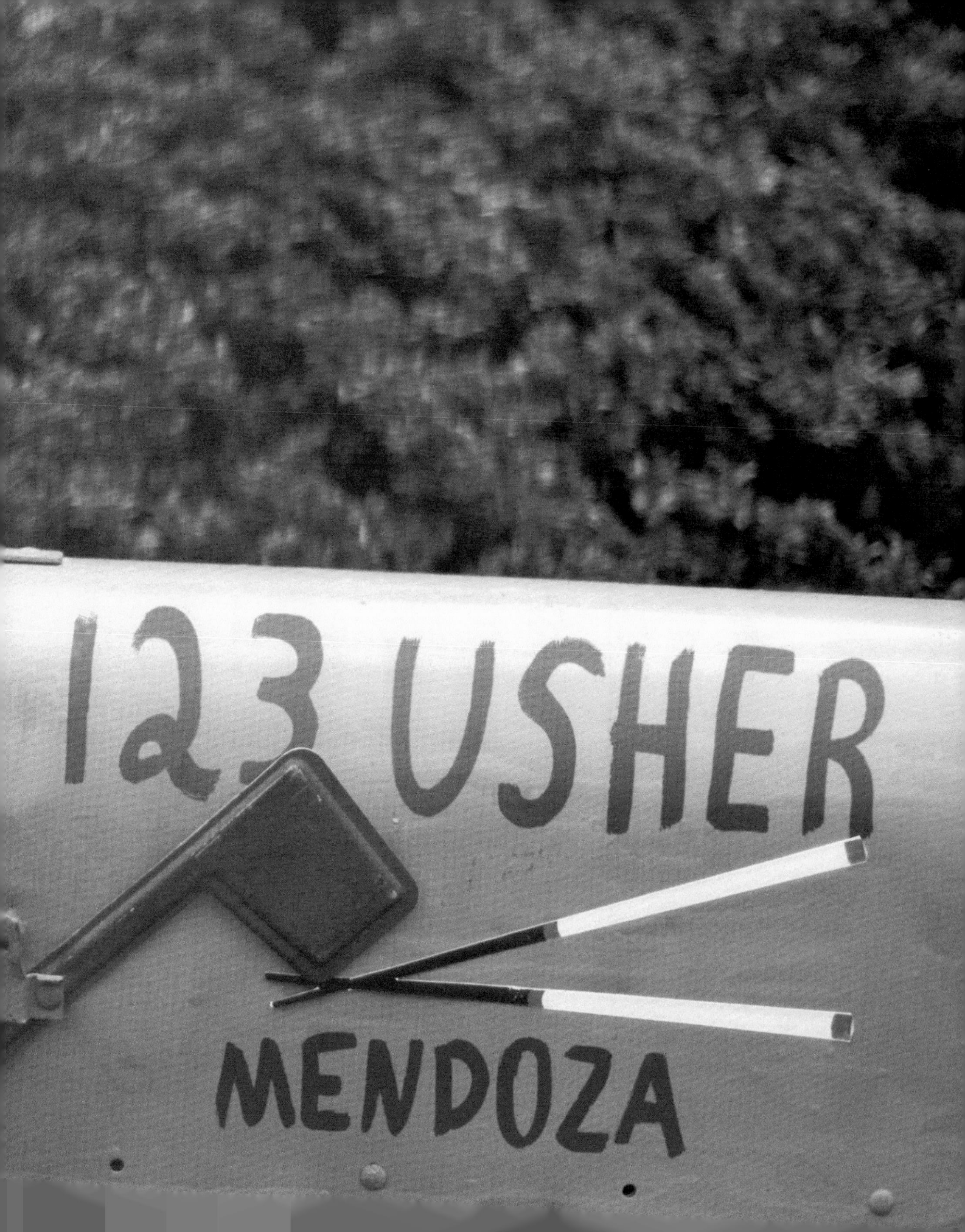
123 USHER
MENDOZA

SHE IS THE Most beautiful girl I have ever seen. She invited me over ~~to play~~ and played Chopin on her piano.

I watched her hands. They looked like ~~giant twigs~~ giant twigs. Like an idiot, I told her I listened to rock music, and all my mother plays all day is maldito Julio Iglesias.

She gave me her music to keep. She didn't need it anymore she said. "It was a gift," she said. "Look at it, and think of me."

HOW can I stop
thinking of her?

Te amo como se aman
ciertas cosa oscuras,
secretamente, entra la
sombra y el alma...

10/31

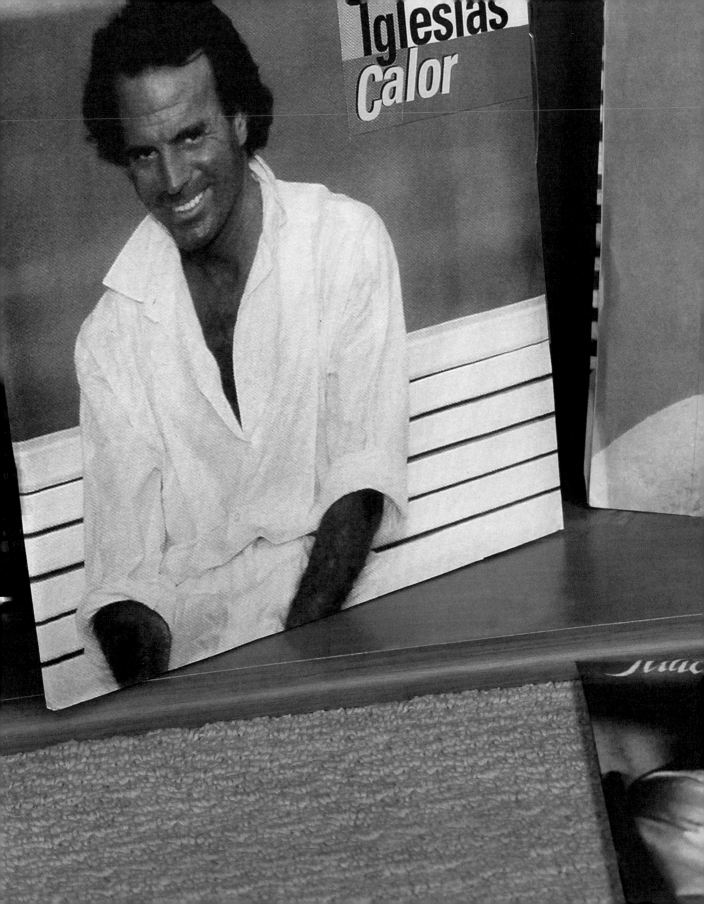

"...un canto a Galicia que es mi tierra madre..."

The 24 Greatest Songs

Frank's Fav...

Here's your Kiss, Frank.

Me and
Francisco.
Nov. 24, 2007

It's the Argentinian middleweight champion, Sergio "The Marvel" Martinez! Quote of the day: "Professional boxers don't wear three kinds of plaid." -G

190

Animalium Mar. Ordo XIII.

nostra Polypum parte prona repræsentat ea uerò quam *Rondeletius* dedit, partem quæ corrue-
enciari ſupinam geminas acetabulorum ordines eleganter exprimit.

1. July, July - The Decemberists

2. Us - Regina Spektor

3. Let's Get out of this Country - Camera Obscura

4. Marching Bands of Manhattan - Death Cab for Cutie

5. The Greatest - Cat Power

6. Gideon - My Morning Jacket

7. New Slang - The Shins

8. Un canto a Galicia - Julio Iglesias

Chat with Chopstixgirl

March 9. 2008. 1:12pm.

Can you see me? I can see your
room from here...

I see you! I'm waving...

I'm making you something

1. LA Balsa - Los Gatos

2. Musica Ligera - Soda Stereo

3. Break It all - Los Shakers

4. Sin Documentos - Los Rodriguez

5. Algo Importante - Billy Bond

6. Quizá's porqué - Sui Generis

7 No Pibe - Maxul

8. El Amor - Julio Iglesias

"Don't get my mother started on wine from Argentina. She says it's the best thing in the world for growing boys. *El mejor*. 'It calms them down,' she says. 'Prevents sexual impulses.'"

"Frank, stop it! Be serious."

"I am serious! Mendoza vines
are the most frigid in the world.
People cross their legs after
only one glass."

Vines of Mendoza

The Mendoza Province is one of Argentina's most important wine regions, accounting for nearly two-thirds of the country's entire wine production. Located in the eastern foothills of the Andes, in the shadow of Mount Aconcagua, vineyards are planted at the some of the highest altitudes in the world. The principal wine producing areas fall into two main departments-Maipú and Luján which includes Argentina's first delin-eated appellation established in 1993 in Luján de Cuyo. The pink-skinned grapes of Criolla Grande and Cereza account for more than a quarter of all plantings but Malbec is the regions most important planting followed closely by Cabernet Sauvignon, Tempranillo and Chardonnay. Mendoza is considered the heart of the winemaking industry in Argentina with the vast majority of large wineries located in the provincial capital.

Property of W.J. Import/Export

...ality Since 1869

Property of W.J. Import/Export

Date: June 25, 2008

Student: Francisco Mendoza

Year: 2007-2008

REPORT CARD	
CLASS	**GRADE**
ESL	B-
American History	D
Geometry	C
Biology	D
Music	B-
Phys Ed	F
Art	A
Choir	C

COMMENTS:

While Frank's improvements in English as a Second Language, Music and Choir are significant, low marks remain in several subjects. We feel Frank would benefit from weekly independent meetings with one of our special learning service teachers. Frank's achievement in art is admirable; however, his reluctance to participate in physical education is a grave concern. It is important that we work together to explain the health benefits of regular exercise and movement to Frank. As you know, there is no soccer program at Willard Dunn, but we feel that games like basketball, tennis and bombardment are just as exciting, and hope that Frank makes more of an effort in this department soon. There is no merit in standing in the center of the gym and not moving, allowing oneself to be hit by the ball, and spending the rest of the game on the sidelines. We feel this does not boost a young man's character or general well-being, and certainly does not encourage the Willard Dunn spirit of teamwork and collaboration. We hope Frank will try harder in the fall.

LOCAL NEWS

"Brecht of the Piano" to Tour Europe

It was only a matter of time. From the Bronx to Brussels, our very own Gloria Fleming is scheduled to embark upon her first international tour. Ms. Fleming is slated to headline several orchestras for performances in Germany, Belgium, Spain, France, Italy, Russia and elsewhere. Her father, Victor, has enrolled Ms. Fleming in an American school in Florence where she will continue her studies, but most of the sixteen-year-old's time will be spent performing in locales as grand as the Festhalle in Frankfurt, Germany, the Voorst Nationale in Brussels, Belgium, and the Palais Omnisports de Paris-Bercy in Paris, France. A far cry from Usher Avenue. –*H.M.*

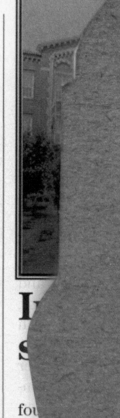

I
S

fou
dar
the
loca
to b
date
mayo
espe
please

CHAPTER 4

Ami Swanson Music Photography

345 E. 81st Street, Apt. 5A
New York, NY 10028

ph: (212) 363-1540 / fax: (212) 363-1541

aswanson@photolabsnyc.com

Chat with Chopstixgirl

August 4, 2008. 2:43pm

Are you really going?

I am

when do you leave?

This fall

how long are you gone?

A year. There's this
school in Italy...

Florence

It sounds OK

i have to see you. tonite.

I know—but we can't.

August 4, 2008. 2:45pm

this is crazy. i'm coming over now…

DON'T!!!! V is in next room.

meet me at our place. i'll be there in 5

"Oh, you're changing your heart...
Oh, you know who you are..."

are you there?

Yeah

what did he say?

We leave tomorrow

i can't fucking believe it

He won't listen. There's nothing I can do. I told him I didn't want to go.

I hate him!!!!!

want me to come over?

i don't think so

August 29, 2008. 9:22pm

i'm coming over

It's not a good idea

i don't care

Nothing can happen, understand?

nothing will happen.
i need you.

V says we're too young.
He doesn't like you
you know that

i don't give a shit. he doesn't
know you. he doesn't know
his own daughter. i'm
coming over. i'll bring a movie

August 29, 2007. 9:23pm

Use basement door

PRODUCCIONES ANHELO presenta

Y TU MAMÁ TAMBIÉN

una película de ALFONSO CUARÓN

B.S.O INCLUYE TEMAS DE
MOLOTOV vs. DUB PISTOLS
EAGLE EYE CHERRY
PLASTILINA MOSH y TONINO CAROTONE con CHALE DE VOLODIMIR
TITÁN y LA MALA RODRÍGUEZ
y muchos más...

MARIBEL VERDÚ   GAEL GARCÍA BERNAL   DIEGO LUNA

JORGE VERGARA · PRODUCCIONES ANHELO presenta "Y TU MAMÁ TAMBIÉN" MARIBEL VERDÚ · GAEL GARCÍA BERNAL · DIEGO LUNA DIRECTOR DE REPARTO MANUEL TEIL
VESTUARIO GABRIELA DIAQUE SUPERVISIÓN MUSICAL LIZA RICHARDSON ANETTE FRADERA EDICIÓN ALFONSO CUARÓN · ALEX RODRÍGUEZ DIRECTOR DE ARTE MIGUEL ÁLVAREZ
DIRECTOR DE PRODUCCIÓN SANDRA SOLARES DIRECTOR DE FOTOGRAFÍA EMMANUEL LUBEZKI PRODUCTORES EJECUTIVOS SERGIO AGÜERO · DAVID LINDE · AMY KAUFMAN
PRODUCIDA POR JORGE VERGARA ESCRITA POR CARLOS CUARÓN DIRIGIDA POR ALFONSO CUARÓN

ANHELO   music plus es SOGEPAQ

"We don't have to say anything..."

LONDON

CHAPTER 5

ENGLAND

I got my birthday presents. They are too beautiful to open, F. Are they paintings? I am imagining they're paintings of our last night together...

Think of me.

-G

F

123

Bronx

Air Mail

Mendoza

er Avenue

10456 USA

Air Mail

Frank Mendoza

23 Usher Avenue

Bronx, NY 10456

USA

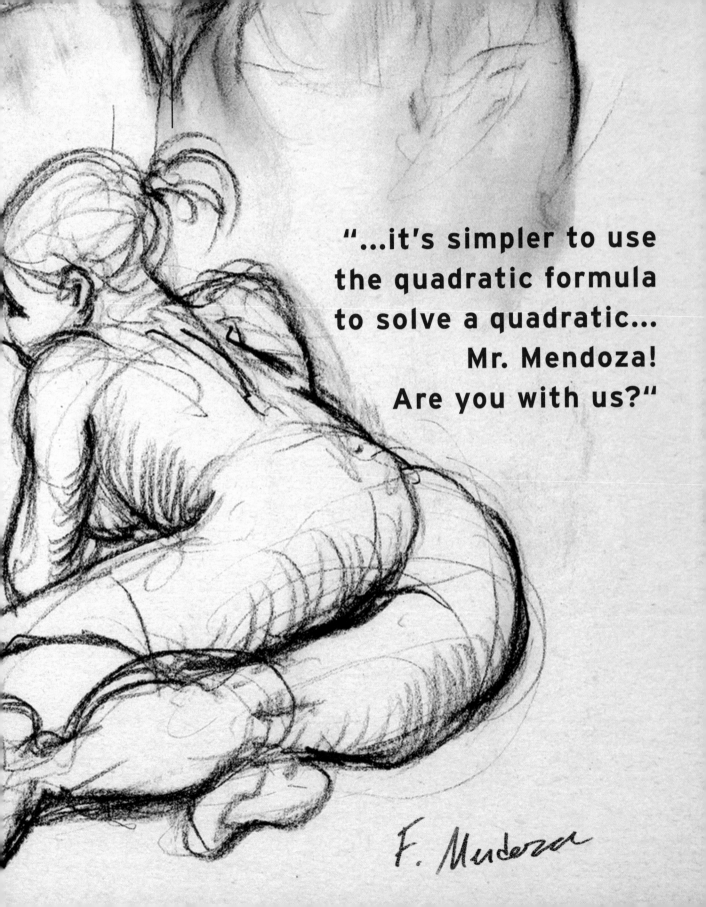

"...it's simpler to use the quadratic formula to solve a quadratic... Mr. Mendoza! Are you with us?"

Chat with Chopstixgirl

October 1, 2008. 4:12am.

are you thinking of me?

Always

where are you? are you
ever coming back???

Brussels. The Vorst Nationaal.

October 1, 2008. 4:13am.

what did you play?

Beethoven. But something
weird happened

what?

I thought of you

why is that weird?

I wanted to play Chopsticks

that's not weird

I DID it, F. I don't know what
happened. I just played it

victor must be pissed

Chat with Chopstixgirl

October 1, 2008. 4:14am.

Victor IS pissed

i love that you did it. maybe
if you keep playing it you can
come home. i miss you so
much.my heart is exploding
(poof)

you still there?

Yes...sorry...V came in and
yelled at me to go to sleep

without you, NYC is like
drinking old man's piss

after a bottle of red wine

y los asparragos

Asparagus is disgusting

when are you back?
seriously...

F,

Desperately missing you!!! Don't
know what I would do without IM.
But it's just not the same. I try
to write more but Victor's watching
me practically every second.
I walked down town by myself today
to see the Basillica and when I
got back he totally freaked.
Last week I asked him if we could
get a moped and he didn't speak
to me for a whole day. I am in
prison!! Send me a piece
of you? -G

Frank Mendoza

123 Usher Avenue

Bronx, NY 10456 USA

postaprioritaria
Priority Mail

NEW ZEALAND

MONDAY EVENING, FEBRUARY 15, 1890,
AT 8.15 O'CLOCK.

(Under the Auspices of the UNIVERSITY MUSICAL SOCIETY.)

PADEREWSKI'S

PIANO RECITAL,

For the Benefit of the Woman's Annex to the WATERMAN GYMNASIUM.

PROGRAMME.

SONATA APPASSIONATA,	Beethoven
PAPILLONS,	Schumann
ERL-KING,	Schubert-Liszt
NOCTURNE,)	
ETUDE	Chopin
...	
CHOPSTICKS,	Allen
MELODIE,)	
MENUET,	Paderewski
HOCHZEITSMARSCH und ELFENREIGEN,	Mendelssohn-Liszt

Steinway & Sons' Pianos used at these Recitals.

Tickets to holders of Choral Union tickets, 50 cents; to persons
not holding Choral Union tickets, 75 cents.

For Sale at Ann Arbor Organ Co.'s Music Store; Calkin's Drug Store and
at Sabin's Drug Store, Ypsilanti, and at Hall on evening of Concert.

ANTON RUBINSTEIN'S new book, entitled: "A Conversation on Music," trans-
lated for the author by Mrs. John P. Morgan, has just been published. Price,
cloth, $1.00. Copyright 1892. For sale by all booksellers and music-dealers, or
mailed upon receipt of price.

LOVE IS WILD
AND WHEN IT IS CUT
RETURNS AGAIN, STRONGER
WHETHER YOU WANT IT TO
OR NOT
—F

F. Mendoza
123 Usher Avenue
Bronx, NY 11951

The International School of Florence
Villa Le Tavernule-via del Caruta, 23/25
50012 Bagno a Ripoli, Italy

LOVE IS WILD
AND WHEN IT IS CUT
RETURNS AGAIN, STRONGER
WHETHER YOU WANT IT TO
OR NOT

—F

Let's Learn English!

Worksheet 27.3: CAREERS

Instructions: Copy the sentences below.

1. **Having a job in America is important.**

   Having a job in America is Important.

2. **If I work hard, my boss will give me a raise.**

   If I work hard, My boss will give me a raise

3. **Being a good citizen is important in the workplace.**

   Being a good citizen is important in the workplace

4. **In America, I can be anything. I can be a cook or a gardener, for example.**

   In America, I can be anything, I can be an artist or a mad man, for example.

5.

My grandfather loves picking it up, but he is getting older.

My Grandfather died in 1983. It was Alzheimer's.

6. **My sister has a new, exciting career as a nurse.**

My sister has a new exciting career as a part figgion.

7. **I always eat lunch at my desk.**

Eating fills me with sorrow.

8. **In the workplace, it is best to arrive early and leave late.**

In the workplace, it is best to wear fur shoes and a penis thong

9. **The boss is always right.**

The boss is always a dumb white castrato with a stupid glim.

10. **For job security, I do everything required of me.**

For job security, I jump on my desk and stick out my elbows

like wings. I fly from desk to desk, kicking over computers...

I forester quilledo!!

MADISON SQUARE GARDEN

A section **6** row **7** seat

October 16, 2008

Enter TOWER C Gate 2

MADISON SQUARE GARDEN
NEW YORK CITY

Heavyweight Championship of the World

SERGIO 'THE MARVEL' MARTINEZ

vs.

BILLY 'THE MANIAC' BUXTON

October 16th, 2008

Ringside 35.00

A section **6** row **7** seat

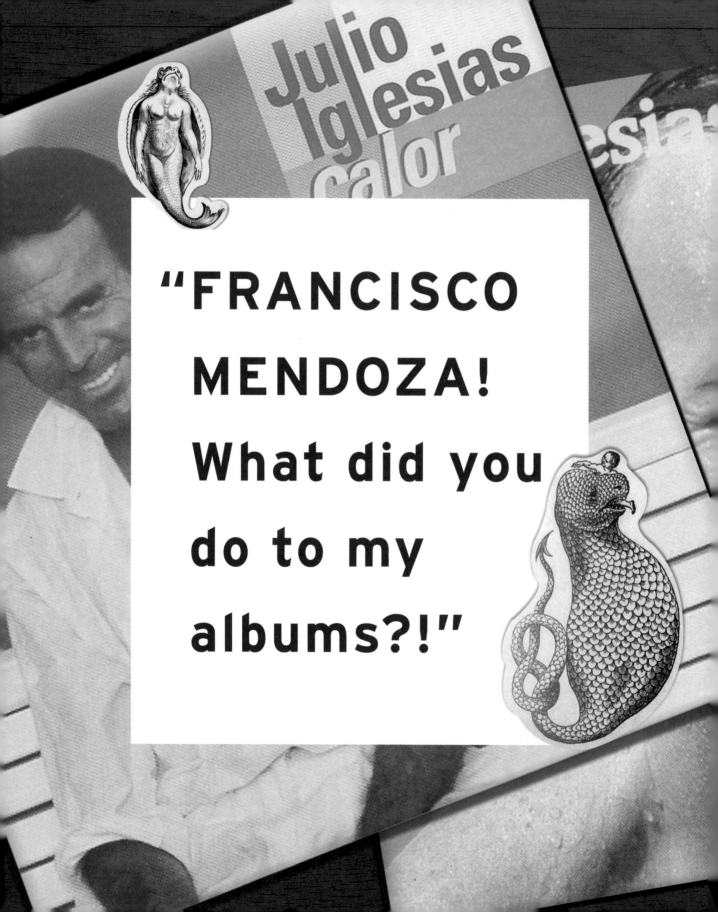

"FRANCISCO MENDOZA! What did you do to my albums?!"

e 24 Greatest Songs

Postcard (top):

Sick and miserable. We had to cancel two concerts and V is brooding in the next room. I've got this one tiny TV that looks like Soviet spacecraft from the 1950s or something. Right now it's showing a Romanian movie with German subtitles and a Russian voice over.

Where are you??!!

Postmark: MOSCOW NOV.15 2008 RUSSIA

ADDRESS

Fran

123 (

Bron

Air

Postcard (underneath, left):

I finally pu
told Victor
Is the
than
's like F,
de of   you wo
city is ali
explain. He
on the Karlovy Most with my arm wrapped around a statue and stared at the artists who sell their paintings over the Vltava.

Frank M
123 Ushe
Bronx, N
USf

POSTCARD

V loves it here. The sky, the fish, the people. I can see why. But without you, everything is empty or broken. It's just how I feel.

OSLOW
NOV 27
2008
NORWAY

NO.
NOR
200

550

Frank M
123 Usher
Bronx, NY
USA

Flu is gone, but I'm s
coughing. V is excited because
they changed venues to the
biggest in Vilnius—the Concert
Hall— and they sold out. He said
today that we're coming back
soon... maybe for the
holidays?! I hope so. You
have no idea how much
I miss you, F. Don't Forget.

Frank Mendoza
123 Usher Avenue
Bronx, NY 10456
USA

Air Mail

December 3, 2008. 4:19am.

¿piensa en mí?

Every night I think of you. Every night I close my eyes and think of you in your attic. I think of you sitting at your desk. I miss looking at you. I miss my heart.

your heart misses you.

look what i saw on TV
"http://www.youtube.com/watch
?v=lhF4gu87rn0"

chopsticks!

"http://www.youtube.com/ watch?v=J1gAHil89Z4"

look what i can do
"http://www.youtube.com/watch ?v=CjuhB1GBX5k"

BRAVO!!

keep thinking of me, glory. write me. Te quiero, Diente de león…

SOLD

Date: December 21, 2008

Student: Francisco Mendoza

Year: Fall 2008

REPORT CARD	
CLASS	**GRADE**
ESL	D
European History	F
Trigonometry	D+
Chemistry	F
Phys Ed	F
Art	A
Choir	B-

COMMENTS:
Please schedule a meeting with us as soon as possible. Frank is proving to be a fine artist, but there is little else to his academic record that demonstrates merit. On top of this, Frank's behavior in school is becoming more and more aggressive. We are concerned for his safety and well-being. There is a strong possibility that Frank is just not Willard Dunn material. Over eighty-five percent of Willard Dunn boys graduate with college acceptances at top schools. At this rate, there is little expectation that Frank will be able to attend college. We recommend that you begin seeking out art or trade schools sooner rather than later in your area which might become a better fit for Frank. But we can discuss all of the above in detail at our meeting. On a side note, we wish Frank a good deal of luck at our winter art auction.

SOLD

F. Muderson

F. Muderson

NOT
FOR
SALE

"Unsere Silvesterparty wäre ohne das Ragtime-Klavier von Jo Ann Castle komplett..."

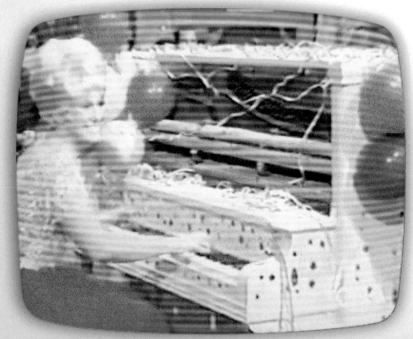

"Our New Year's Eve party wouldn't be complete without the ragtime piano of Jo Ann Castle..."

CHAPTER 6

F~

I'm so sorry I haven't written. It happened again. I slipped into Chopsticks at the Royal Albert in London, and now V won't let me out of his sight. He says I've been on the computer too much, and took it away from me. We're back in Germany. He's got me seeing this awful doctor in Berlin. She clears her throat every other word. I hate her!! V says we're coming home in a few weeks, but I don't believe him. I honestly don't know when I'll see you, F. Everyone is <u>lying</u> to me...

JUSTUS von LIEBIG   12. MAI 1803

DEUTSCHE BUNDESPOST 30

L. SCHNELL

Air Mail

Frank Mendoza

123 Usher Avenue

Bronx, NY 10456

USA

WILLARD DUNN SCHOOL FOR BOYS
1500 Waters Place · Bronx, NY 10461 · (718) 862-3004 · fax: (718) 862-9987

Feb. 13, 2009

Official Notice of Suspension

Name: FRANCISCO MENDOZA

Date Issued: 2/13/2009

Date of Occurrence: 2/13/2009

Length of Suspension: 2/16–2/18/2009

Reason for Suspension: Fighting during gym class

Further Comments:

Mr. & Mrs. Mendoza,

We clean the lockers of all suspended students. Enclosed please find the contents of Frank's locker. We remind you to speak with Frank about smoking on school grounds, and we are obviously concerned that he has become sexually active.

Frank has been suspended for fighting. When Gerald Babbitt, our gym instructor, tried to break up the fight, Frank said, "Tu hermano no tiene testículos."

Mr. Babbitt does not speak Spanish, but that's besides the point. This is unacceptable behavior. Please advise your son that if he does not change his behavior and respect authority, there may be drastic consequences.

Sincerely,

Principal

FRANCISCO MENDOZA,

YOU ARE NO LONGER

MI HIJO PEQUEÑO.
YOU'll WIN NEXT TIME

PAPA

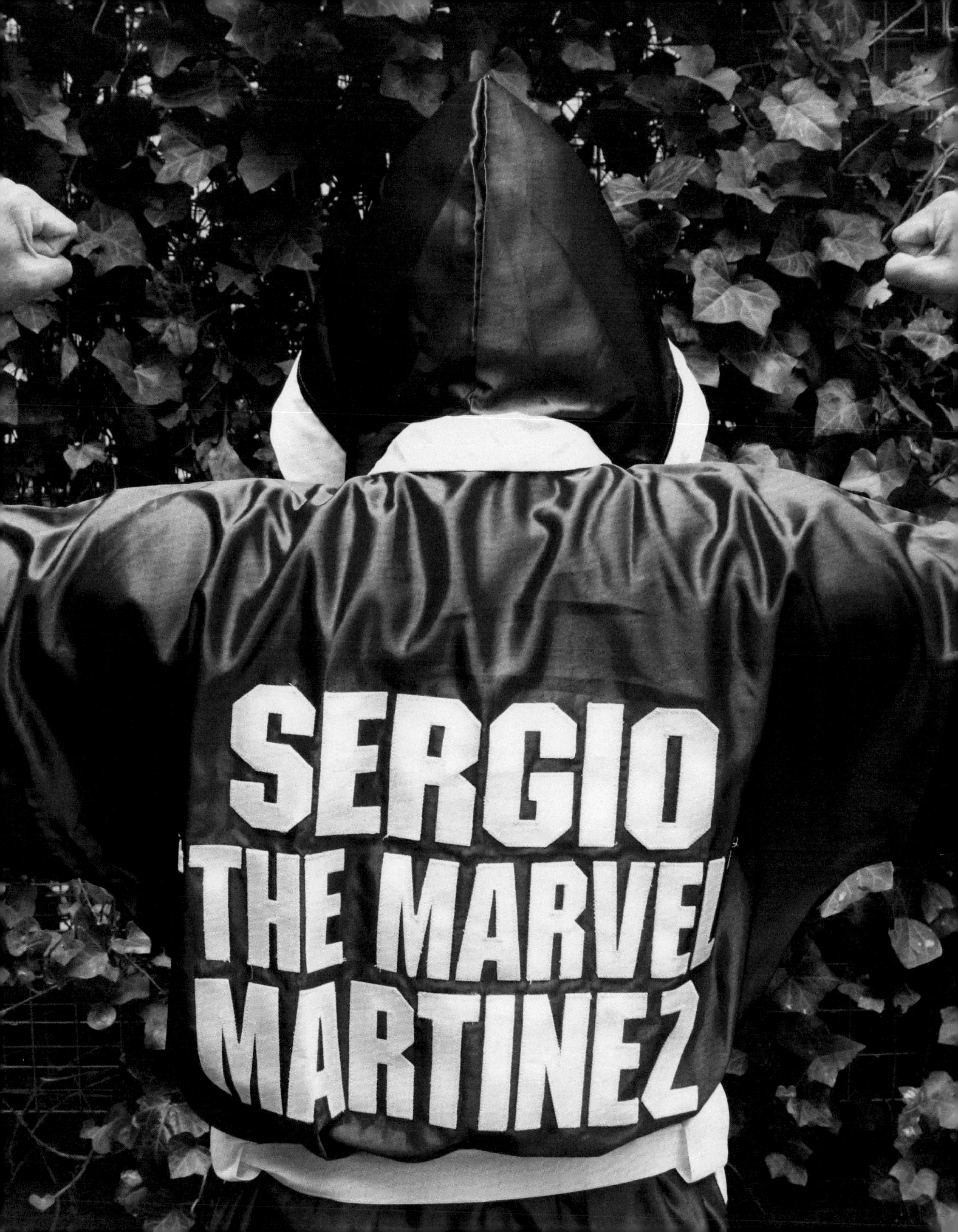
SERGIO
THE MARVEL
MARTINEZ

Are you there?

It happened again.
We're coming home.

Feb. 18, 2009. 11:59pm

Are you there?

http://www.youtube.com/watch?v=qaMcImrNnOQ

are you thinking of me?

always

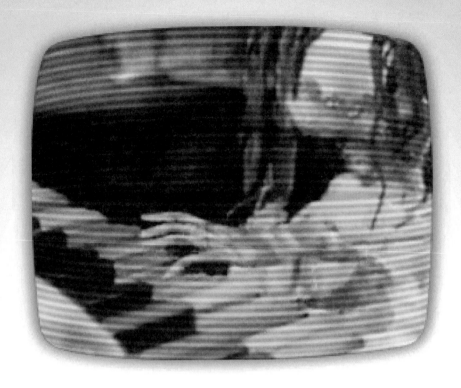

virgin atlantic ~~Virgin~~

i ECONOMY CLASS

USCITA / GATE | POSTO / SEAT

32 14A

NON-FUMATORI
NO SMOKING

DESTINAZIONE / TO

NEW YORK CITY/JFK

PASTO / MEAL

NORMALE

NOME / NAME

FLEMING/VICT

POSTO / SEAT | CLASSE /

14A E

▶ 17:30

DESTINAZIONE / TO

NEW YOR

OSSERVAZIONI /

be having shock treatments three times a week—Tuesday, Thursday and Saturday."

I gulped in a long draught of air.

"For how long?"

"That depends," Doctor Nolan said, "on you and me."

I took up the silver knife and cracked off the cap of my egg. Then I put down the knife and looked at it. I tried to think what I had loved knives for, but my mind slipped from the noose of the thought and swung, like a bird, in the center of empty air.

Joan and DeeDee were sitting side by side on the piano bench, and DeeDee was teaching Joan to play the bottom half of "Chopsticks" while she played the top.

I thought how sad it was Joan looked so horsey, with such big teeth and eyes like two gray, goggly pebbles. Why, she couldn't even keep a boy like Buddy Willard. And DeeDee's husband was obviously living with some mistress or other and turning her sour as an old fusty cat.

"I've got a let-ter," Joan chanted, poking her tousled head inside my door.

"Good for you." I kept my eyes on my book. Ever since the shock treatments had ended, after a brief series of five, and I had town privileges, Joan hung about me like a large and breathless fruitfly—as if the sweetness of recovery were something she could suck up by mere nearness. They had taken away her physics books and the piles of dusty spiral pads full of lecture notes that had fringed her room, and she was confined to grounds again.

"Don't you want to know who it's *from?*"

Joan edged into the room and sat down on my bed. I

Frank Mendoza ♥

wanted to tell her to get the hell out, she gave me the creeps, only I couldn't do it.

"All right." I stuck my finger in my place and shut the book. "Who from?"

Joan slipped out a pale blue envelope from her skirt pocket and waved it teasingly.

"Well, isn't that a coincidence!" I said.

"What do you mean, a coincidence?"

I went over to my bureau, picked up a pale blue envelope and waved it at Joan like a parting handkerchief. "I got a letter too. I wonder if they're the same."

"He's better," Joan said. "He's out of the hospital."

There was a little pause.

"Are you going to marry him?"

"No," I said. "Are you?"

Joan grinned evasively. "I didn't like him much anyway."

"Oh?"

"No, it was his family I liked."

"You mean Mr. and Mrs. Willard?"

"Yes." Joan's voice slid down my spine like a draft. "I loved them. They were so nice, so happy, nothing like my parents. I went over to see them all the time," she paused, "until you came."

Mr & Mrs Mendoza

"I'm sorry." Then I added, "Why didn't you go on seeing them, if you liked them so much?" & Mrs Mendoza

"Oh, I couldn't," Joan said. "Not with you dating Buddy. It would have looked . . . I don't know, *funny*."

I considered. "I suppose so." Mr & Mrs Mendoza

"Are you," Joan hesitated, "going to let him come?"

"I don't know."

At first I had thought it would be awful having Buddy come and visit me at the asylum—he would probably only come to

Mrs Mendoza

Is this okay?

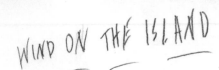

WIND ON THE ISLAND

The wind is a horse:
hear how he runs
through the sea, through the sky.

He wants to take me: listen
how he roves the world
to take me far away.

Hide me in your arms
just for this night,
while the rain breaks
against sea and earth
its innumerable mouth.

Listen how the wind
calls to me galloping
to take me far away.

With your brow on my
with your mouth on m
our bodies tied
to the love that
let the wind pas
and not take me a

Let the wind rush
crowned with fou
let it call to me
galloping in the
while I, sunk
beneath your big eyes,
just for the night
shall rest, my love

Pablo
Neruda
Twenty Love
Poems

AND A SONG OF DESPAIR

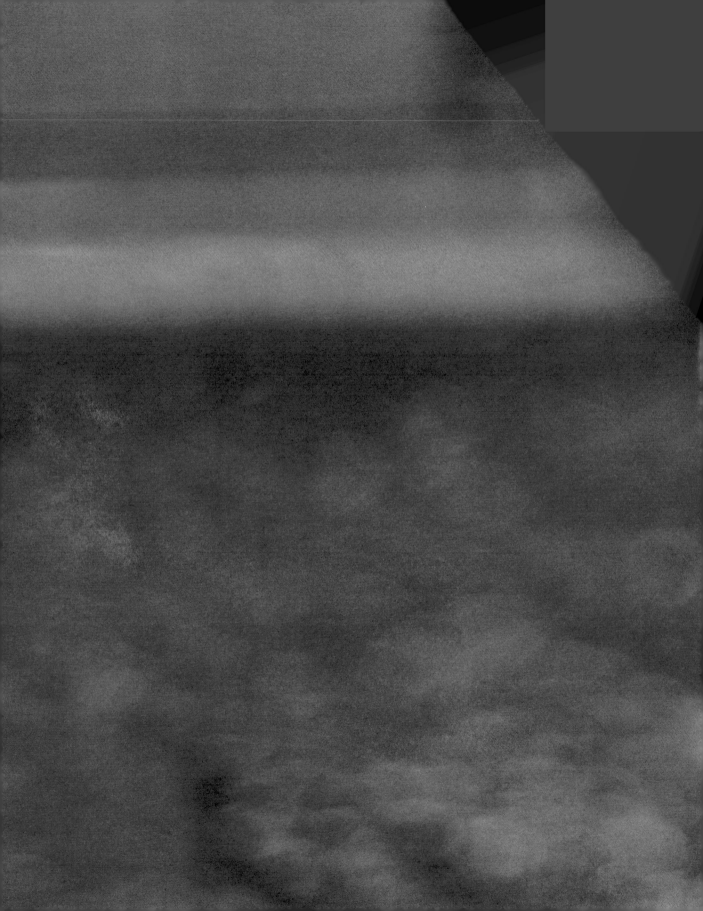

Sweet
Rice

NATURAL BROWN RICE TREATS

dandelion
candy

NET WT 1.75 OZ 50 g

1. Beauty - The Shivers

2. White Winter Hymnal - Fleet Foxes

3. My Imaginary Friend - the Divine Comedy

4. Dandelion - Rolling Stones

5. On the Water - The Walkmen

6. La Respuesta - Los Gatos Salvajes ("The Answer")

7. Your Ex-Lover is Dead - Stars

8. I will Follow You Into the Dark
   - Death Cab For Cutie (piano cover by Gavin Mikhail)

"Time to hear from our queen of the ragtime piano, Jo Ann Castle. Jo Ann, her piano and her friends get into the Easter spirit with this well-known melodium..."

CHAPTER 7

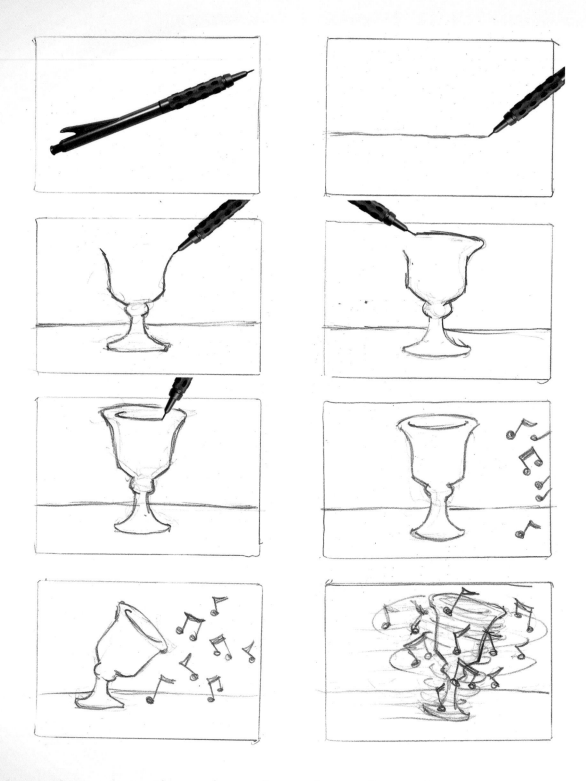

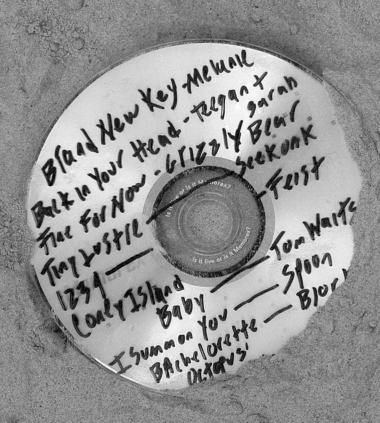

http://www.newyorker.com/

[CG Textures] | Google Maps | YouTube | Wikipedia | Design Blogs▾

THE NEW YORKER

| SUBSCRIBE | IN THE MAGAZINE | BLOGS | AUDIO & VIDEO | LISTINGS | CARTOONS |

THE THEATRE | NIGHT LIFE | ART | DANCE | CLASSICAL MUSIC | MOVIES | READINGS AND TALKS | ABOVE AND BEYOND

THE NEW YORKER | ARTS & CULTURE | EVENTS

GOINGS ON ABOUT TOWN: CLASSICAL MUSIC

BRECHT IN AMERICA: GLORY FLEMING AND THE NEW YORK PHILHARMONIC

Carnegie Hall's grand exploration of European music and arts begins with a concert conducted by Gilbert, the festival's artistic director, and his beloved ensemble. The pianist Glory Fleming is the special guest in a program of works by Beethoven (the Piano Concerto No. 3 in C Minor) and Brahms (The Piano Concerto No. 1 in D Minor).

(212-247-7800. Jul. 17 at 1 p.m.)

Search nev

WELCOME

MOST POPU...

1. News I...
   and Ser...
2. The Bo...
   Fuck to...
3. Debatin...
4. Rationa...
   1930s;
5. Silvio I...

THE MAGAZI...

Table of Con...

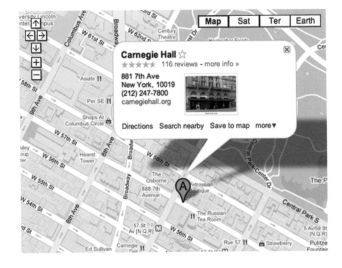

Map | Sat | Ter | Earth

Carnegie Hall ☆
★★★★★ 116 reviews · more info »
881 7th Ave
New York, 10019
(212) 247-7800
carnegiehall.org

Directions   Search nearby   Save to map   more▾

Wish me luck, F

F. Mendoza

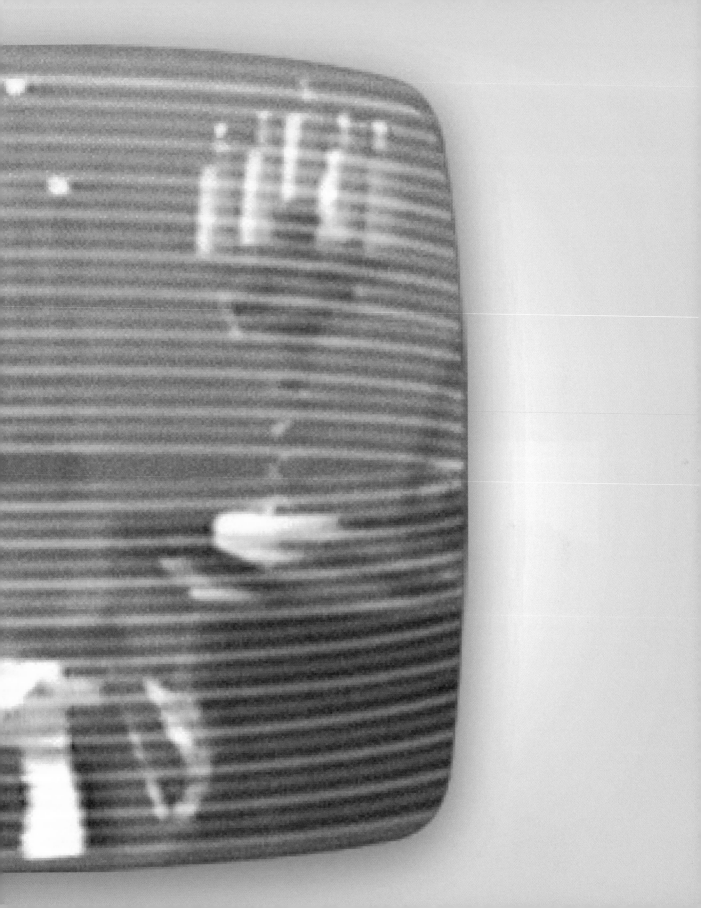

WWW.BXTIMES

BRONX TIMES REPORTER SATURDAY, JULY 18, 2009

What Happened to Gloria Fleming?

By Helen Mundt

(Chapter 8)

Avant-garde is one thing. But last night our own Gloria Fleming, arguably one of the most talented young pianists in the United States and around the globe, stunned a packed audience at Carnegie Hall when she stopped playing mid-performance, and refused to continue.

The concert was apparently going as planned when suddenly, in the middle of the allegro rondo of Brahms' Piano Concerto No. 1, Ms. Fleming lifted her hands from the keys and stopped the performance. Anyone who has experienced the work of Glory Fleming understands that she is known for modernist innovations of classical repertoire, and anticipated one of her famous shifts in genre.

When she resumed playing, however, she disappointed everyone by not performing one of her masterful collages, and instead banging out a frantic and elaborate version of the waltz "Chopsticks," Liberace-style, with dozens of gaudy flourishes.

Members of the New York Philharmonic tried to participate as the conductor looked on, but there was no stopping Ms. Fleming. After she completed the song, she rose from the piano and stood obliquely on stage, staring directly at the audience for several minutes. Finally her father and teacher Victor Fleming ran to her and escorted her off. In hushed tones, the audience filed out quickly thereafter.

For this reporter, the evening was a bizarre disappointment, and no doubt Ms. Fleming's critics will write about the evening with gleeful scorn.

No refunds were issued.

3 County Schools Shut-Down

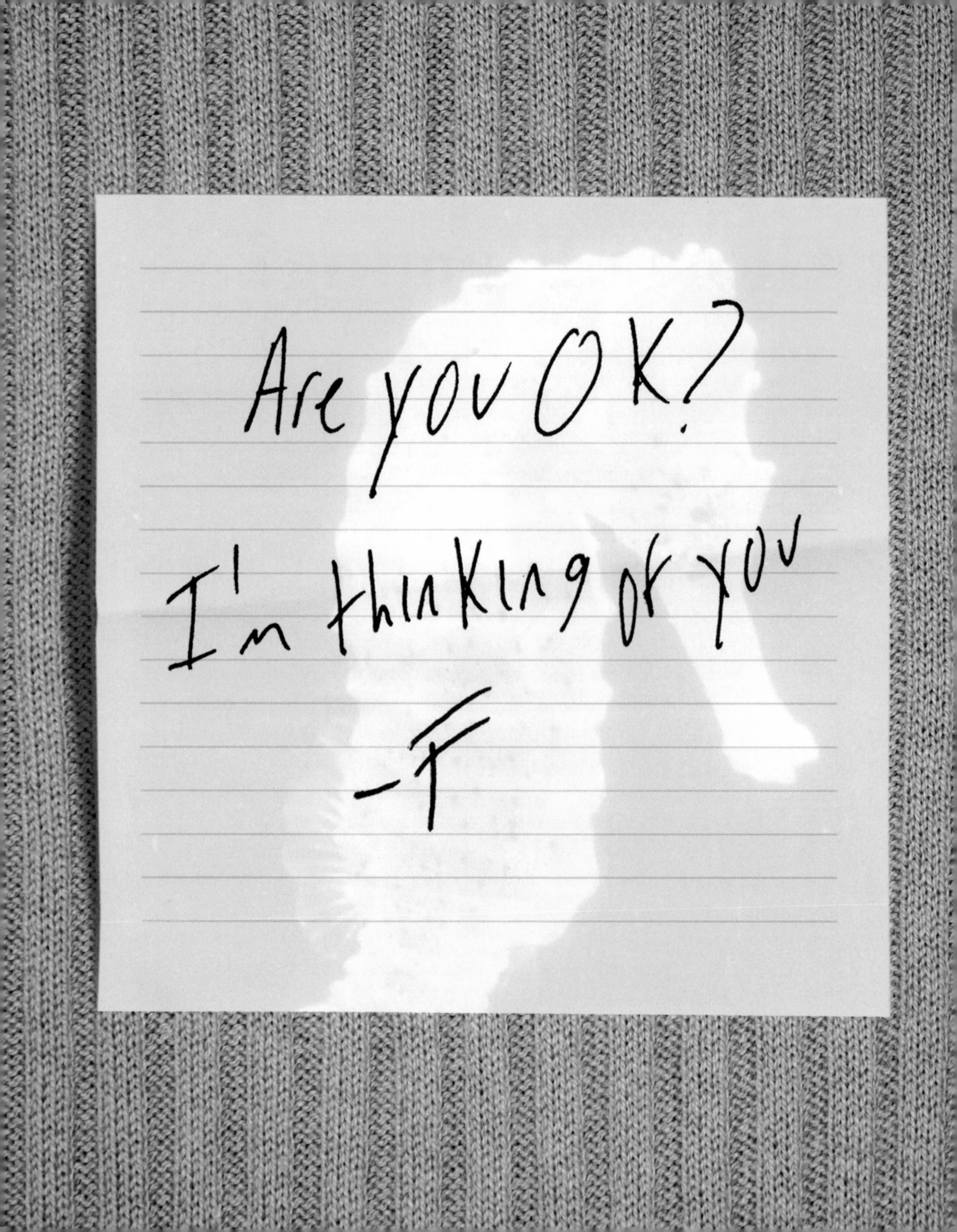
Are you OK?
I'm thinking of you
-F

Chat with Chopstixgirl

July 18, 2009. 11:12pm

you there?

July 18, 2009. 11:14pm

if your there say sthing

your light is on

can you see me? i'm waving

July 19, 2009. 12:05am

why r u ignoring me!?!!!

July 19, 2009. 1:12am

i just need to know you're ok

turn off your light if you're ok

July 19, 2009. 6:40am

your light is still on, mi amor

"I think it's in your mother's old trunk in the bedroom..."

STATE OF NEW YORK

Department of Health
Division of Vital Statistics
Bronx

Certificate of Birth

Gloria Beatrice Fleming

BORN ON:
September 8, 1992
at Bronx, New York

TO PARENTS:
Victor Fleming
(Father)

Maria Torres
(Mother)

WEIGHT:
7 lbs, 10 oz

LENGTH:
21 In.

3015-7475

CIETÉ CIVILE DU DOMAINE DE LA ROMANÉE-CONTI

PROPRIÉTAIRE A VOSNE-ROMANÉE (CÔTE D'OR)

ROMANÉE-CONTI

PPELLATION ROMANÉE-CONTI CONTROLÉE

5.124 Bouteilles R

N. 000363

ANNÉE **1963**

Mise en bouteille au domaine

Wine Spectato
www.winespectato
lifornia Rhônes
ding High
ROBLES SETS THE PACE
BIG RED BLENDS
Value Hot Spot:
Than 100 Wines
85+ for $15 or Less
HONDA

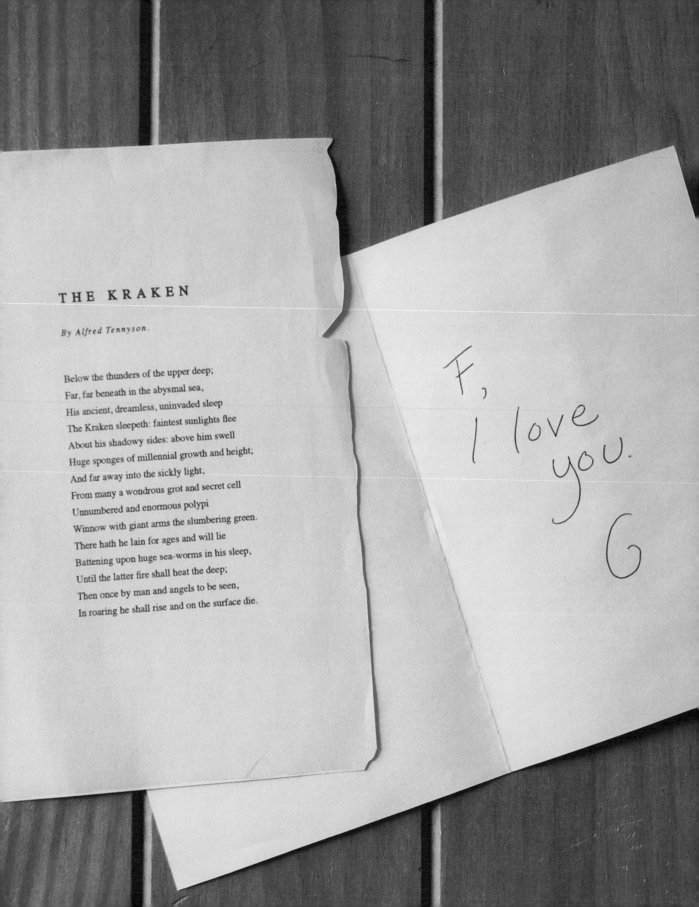

Chat with Chopstixgirl

August 3, 2009. 10:03pm.

> http://www.youtube.com/
> watch?v=GB007OJjP60

There's something wrong with me

> what are you talking about?
> there's nothing wrong with you.
> http://www.youtube.com/
> watch?v=q3m7BZ5tzeg

I can't stop

> stop what?

August 3, 2009. 10:04pm.

Are you there?

http://www.youtube.com/watch?v=ETT3UHEEc1A&feature=related

http://www.youtube.com/watch?v=Vwer8Q4s-AQ

Stop it!!

i'm sorry. i thought you liked it.

I don't! I don't like it at all!

i just want you to think of me

I do think of you

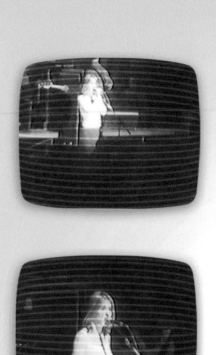

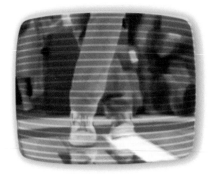

"The Queen of the Ragtime Piano gives us her version of a song the Doughboys were singing back in 1917 ..."

I'm sorry
we fought.
Your heart
loves you
Te amo

"All of these were hers.
Victor stores them wrong..."

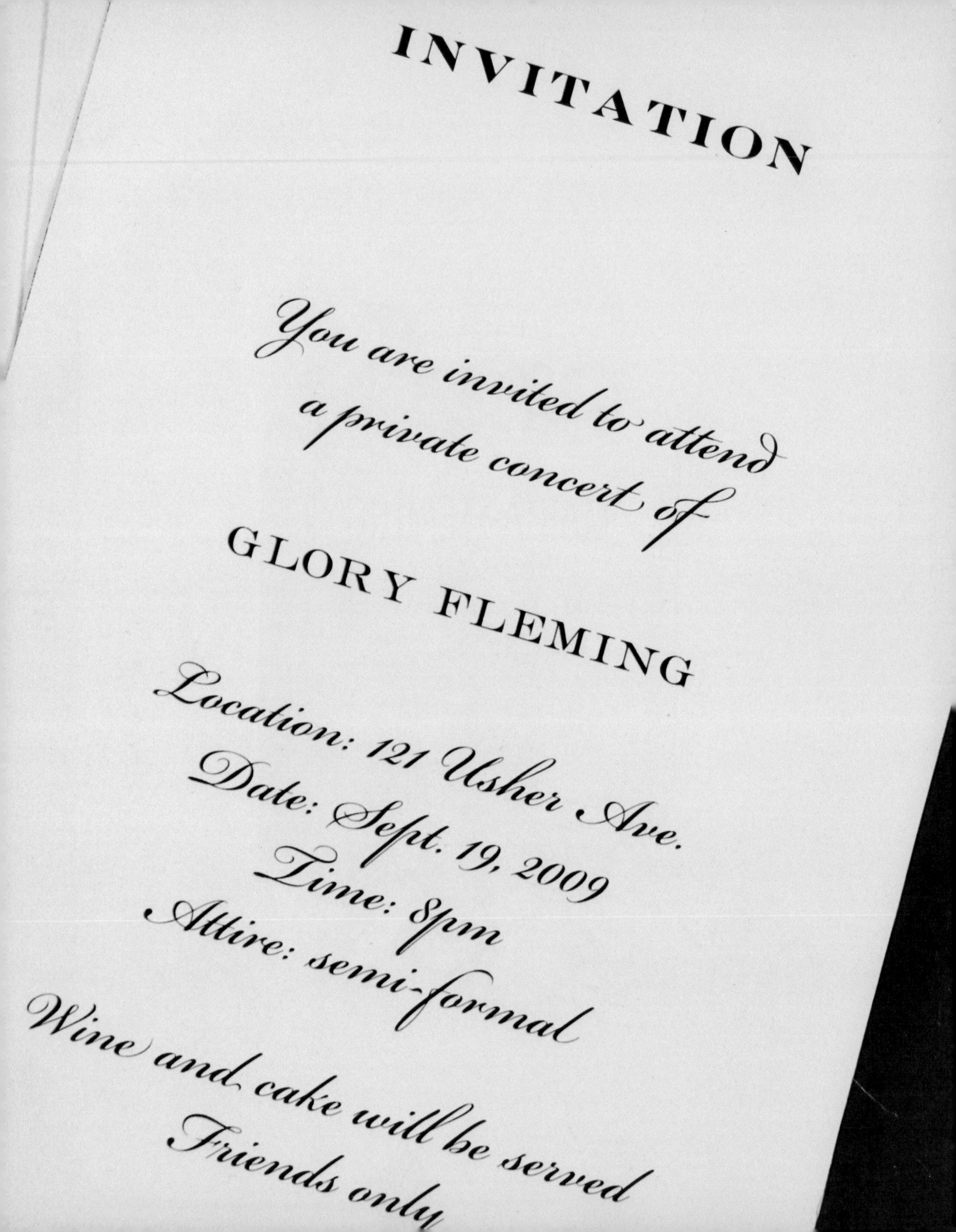

INVITATION

You are invited to attend a private concert of

GLORY FLEMING

Location: 121 Usher Ave.
Date: Sept. 19, 2009
Time: 8pm
Attire: semi-formal

Wine and cake will be served
Friends only

CHAPTER NINE

You are invited to attend
a private concert of

GLORY FLEMING

Location: 121 2...

Please come John.
I need you there

— Victor

"Gloria, you don't have to do
anything you don't want to do.
No one's forcing you to do this.
I've said that all along..."

No, I'll do it...

CONFIRMED GUEST LIST – 15

- MRS EVELYN ANDERSON
  (London symph.)
- ARTHUR AND MIRIAM BOGLE
  (chicago symph.)
- MRS KATHLEEN DARBY + 1
  (glory's former teacher)
- FRED GILBERT AND CHARLES DAWSON
  (NY Phil.)
- MARK AND NEELY HENDERSON
  (San Francisco symph.)
- WES AND BOBBIE MEYERS
  (friend)
- JOHN NICKERSON + 1
  (friend)
- ALEX POSTROVICH (Boston symph.)
- ELIAH SAVAGE + 1 (Met)
- DON AND LINDA URQUIE (friend)

Sept. 18, 2009

Official Notice of Expulsion

Dear Mr. and Mrs. Mendoza,

We regret to inform you that Frank is no longer welcome at the Willard Dunn School for Boys. Our faculty members and staff have tried very hard to work with Frank, and we all recognize his extraordinary talent for the arts. However, it is clear that Frank remains unhappy here, as evidenced by the numerous struggles he has both instigated and endured.

Expulsion is never a first option for any administrator, which is why writing a letter such as this is such a disappointment. However, we do feel that we have tried all we can to make Frank feel at home here. We know that Frank longs to return to a school in Argentina, as it is a desire he has confessed to our art instructor several times. Now that Frank is nearly eighteen, his choices will soon become his own.

It remains our sincere hope that Frank finds whatever it is he's searching for. We wish the Mendoza family nothing but the best of luck.

Sincerely,

Principal

Sept. 18. 2009. 11:10pm.

bad news. Victor says you can't come

why?

You got kicked out of school...

I know it's not your fault

What are you going to do?

estar con ustedes

We can't be together

i'm coming to your show.
you need me there.

No. Victor will KILL you.

who cares? when i'm 18, i'm gone...

What do you mean?

i don't know. back home, maybe

Sept. 18, 2009. 11:11pm

you would leave me?

te vas a venir conmigo!
you can follow me!

Sept. 19, 2009. 2:16am.

I can't sleep. I'm freaking out.
http://www.youtube.com/
watch?v=Bq1HSjZUL5I

Sept. 19, 2009. 2:59am.

are you there?

!?

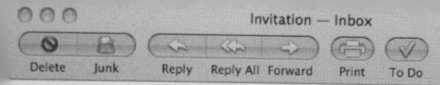
From: John <johnc@gmail.com>
Subject: **Invitation**
Date: Thursday, September 19, 2009 at 10:02 PM EDT
To: Victor Fleming <victorfleming@gmail.com>

Vic,

I'm sorry about tonight. When you said you already lost Maria and were afraid of losing Glory too, I didn't know what you meant.

Now I know.

I tried to stop her from playing—I hope that was the right thing to do. Wasn't it Edison who said that madness is doing the same thing over and over again, and expecting a different result?

At any rate, if you need help with the arrangements, just let me know. Becky and I are here for you, old friend…

J

Strong Fathers, Strong Daughters

10 Secrets Every Father Should Know

GOLDEN HANDS REST FACILITY
1500 Waters Place - Bronx, NY 10461 - (718) 862-3004 - fax: (718) 862-9987

ITEMS TO LEAVE AT HOME
Pets (incl. fish and rodents)
Knives, razors, scissors
Cosmetics
Hair dryers
Plants
OTC medicines
Cigarettes
Alcohol
Computers
Cameras
Cellphones

ITEMS TO PACK
Extra towel
Extra toothbrush
Personal hygiene
Pens and notebooks
Personal music
Arts & crafts

GOLDEN HANDS REST FACILITY
1500 Waters Place - Bronx, NY 10461 - (718) 862-3004 - fax: (7

FORMAL ADMITTANCE RECORD

Name	Admittance
GLORIA FLEMING	
	1/Sep.15, 2001
	2/Jun.27, 2003
	3/Sep. 11, 2004
	4/Mar.4, 2005
	5/Mar.19, 2006
	6/Aug.1, 2007
	7/Nov. 7, 2007
	8/Jan.19, 2008
	9/May 2, 2008
	10/Jul

I'm fighting for you

Love, Dad

CHAPTER 10

CROSSWORD GAME

The "p

IFE®

C

ATION®

SKI
CA

GOLDEN HANDS REST FACILITY
1500 Waters Place - Bronx, NY 10461 - (718) 862-3004 - fax: (718) 862-9987

<u>Week 8 Progress Report</u>

November 15, 2009

Dear Mr. Fleming,

Glory appears to be doing just fine. She is eating regularly and sleeps through the night. She has also made a friend, I am happy to report, and the girls enjoy sewing and watching television together. However she insists on practicing far more than the two hours we usually recommend. After breakfast, Glory will usually disappear into one of our practice rooms, and not re-emerge until dinnertime.

Also, a member of our staff has informed me that Glory only plays Chopsticks, and that she will play the song, in various incarnations, for hours every day. I realize that Glory's stay here has been for much longer than usual, but I recommend that she remain with us through the holidays.

Please contact me if you have any questions about this arrangement.

Sincerely,

Willard Dunn
Chief Administrator

PROPERTY OF GOLDEN HANDS REST FACILITY
Helena Bonham Carter
Johnny Depp
TIM BURTON'S

G. Fleming

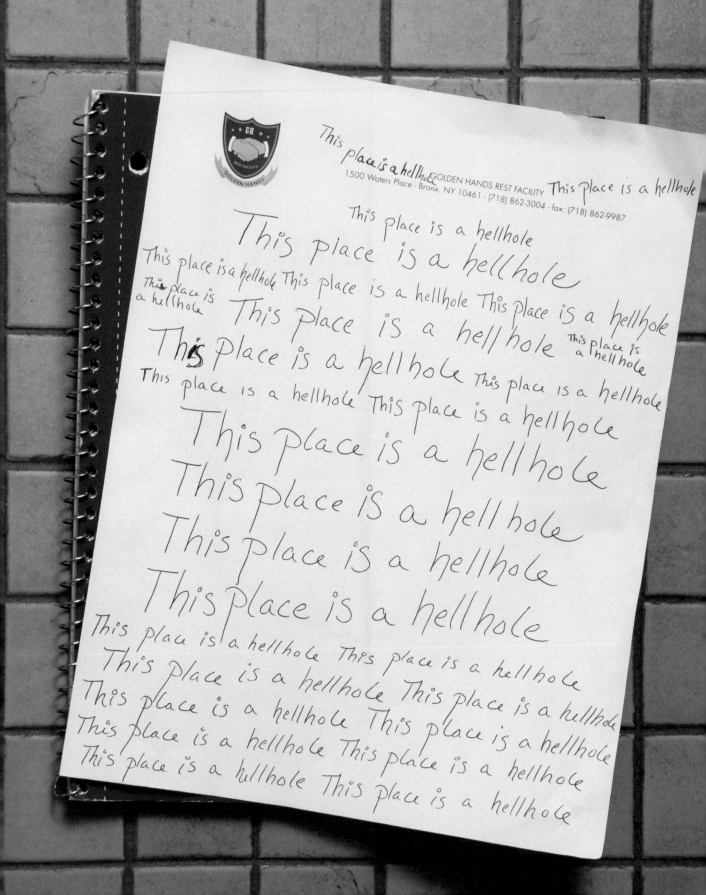

"Good morning. Today is December fifth. Today is a great day. Today we have a special treat for you. Jo Ann Castle will be joining us for an impromptu concert this afternoon..."

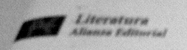

Literatura
Alianza Editorial

New York

THE NEW YORK TIMES

One Night in Moscow

GLORIA
FLEMING

"The Brecht of the Piano"

SOLD
OUT

July 4th, 2007

"...For years, Jo Ann was a regular piano entertainer on the Lawrence Welk Show. So bring your boogie-woogie attitude and join the fun..."

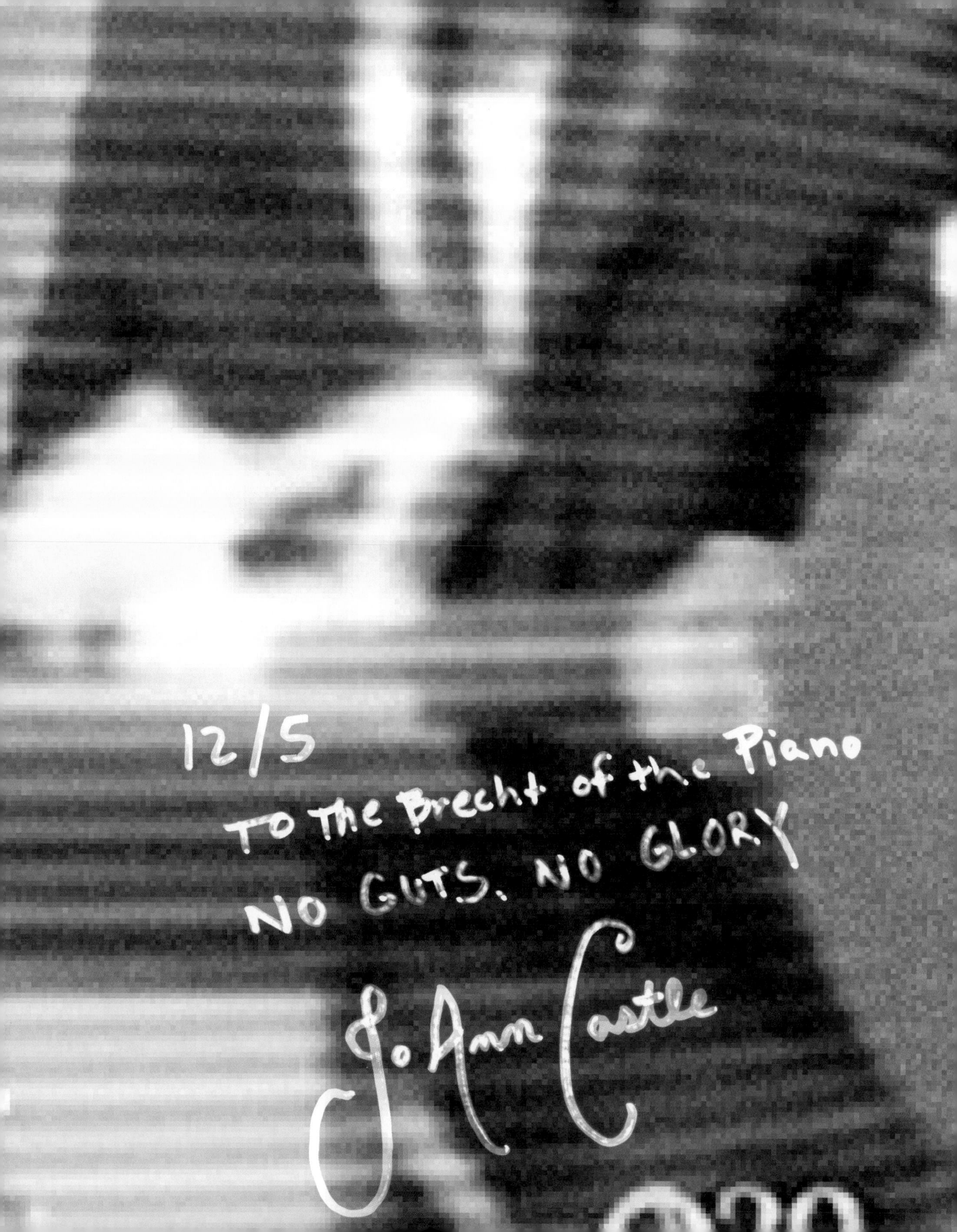

12/5

TO THE Brecht of the Piano

NO GUTS. NO GLORY

JoAnn Castle

"Tonight's main event: a boxing match between Paul "The Punisher" Williams and Sergio "The Marvel" Martinez is being shown in the rec room. All patients and staff are invited to attend..."

IN 75 WEEKLY PARTS/PART 4/VOL 1

EN HANDS REST FACILITY

Golden Hands

essmaking & needlecraft guide

"...Hard right hand and Williams goes down! Martinez has evened the round!...What a savage exchange in the middle of the ring..."

"WILL ALL STAFF MEMBERS PLEASE REPORT TO THE OFFICE IMMEDIATELY. THIS IS NOT A DRILL..."

"ONCE AGAIN, WILL
ALL STAFF MEMBERS
PLEASE REPORT TO THE
OFFICE..."

G. Fleming

G. Fleming

Monograph

By now I'm
I'm sure you know
I've gone.

Can you ever leave that place? If you are thinking of me then follow me.

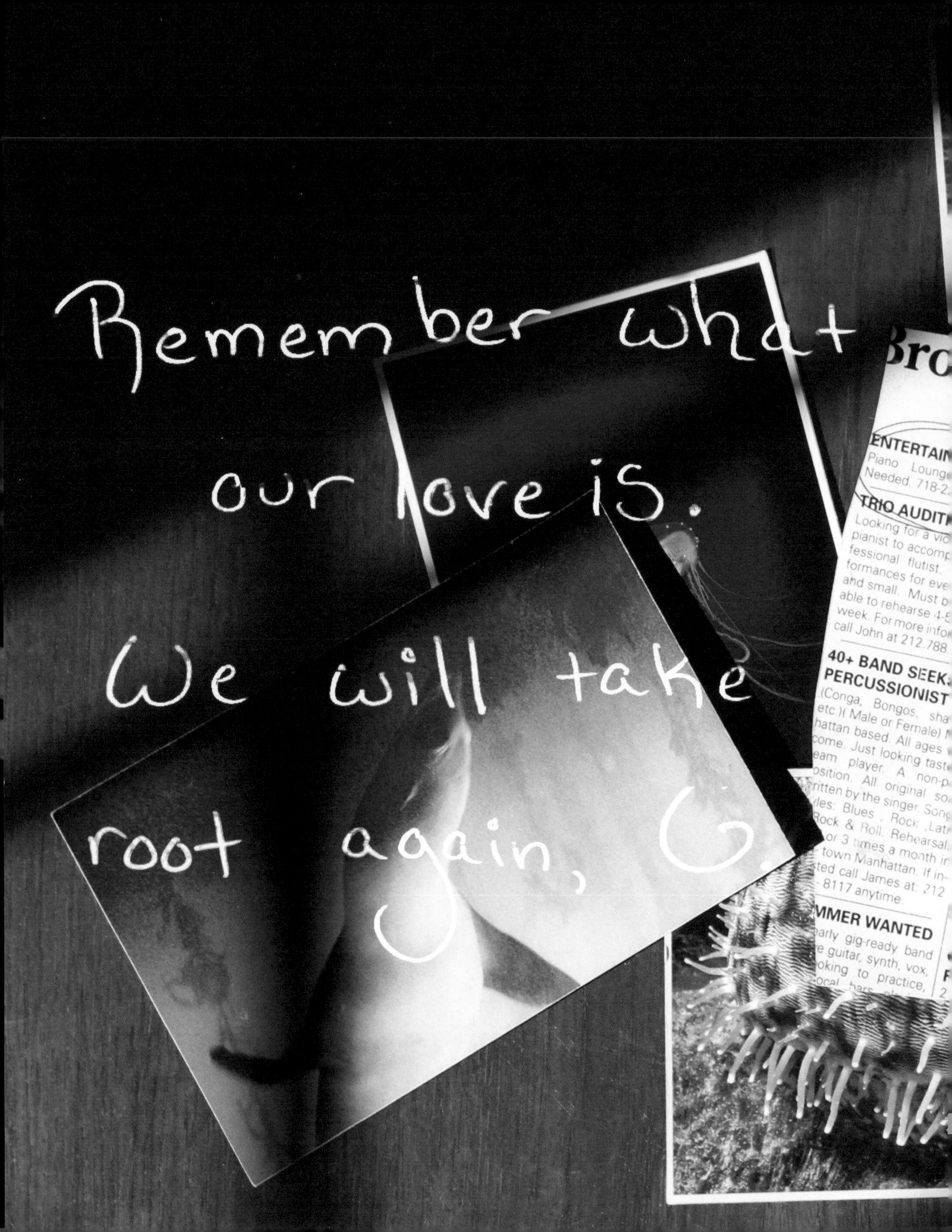
Remember what
our love is.
We will take
root again,
G.

Bronx Times Re

CLASSIFIEDS

ENTERTAINING SEAS

Piano Lounge Performer Needed. 718-223-7133

TRIO AUDITIONS

Looking for a violinist and a pianist to accompany a professional flutist. Paid performances for events, large and small. Must be willing/able to rehearse 4-5 times a week. For more information, call John at 212.788.3344

40+ BAND SEEKS PERCUSSIONIST

(Conga, Bongos, shakers, etc.)(Male or Female) Manhattan based. All ages welcome. Just looking tasteful ___am player. A non-paid ___sition. All original song ___ritten by the singer. Songs ___les: Blues , Rock ,Latin ___ Rock & Roll. Rehearsals ___ 2 or 3 times a month in ___ town Manhattan. If in___ted call James at: 212 ___ 8117 anytime.

___MMER WANTED

___early gig-ready band ___e guitar, synth, vox, ___oking to practice,

GUITAR TEACHER

Skilled guitar teacher for after school kids program needed. Must have experience with children. Teaching credentials a plus.

!TRAVEL THE WORLD FOR YOUR WORK!

Entertain in various locations on board: piano bar, night club etc. (providing your own music and materials) - solid experience and ability to play a wide diversity of musical styles required. Fluent Spanish Language skills required. Salary range: $2500-4800 U.S. per month, plus excellent benefits. Mainly South American ports.
Call Today: 212-588-5680

GUITARIST LOOKING FOR BAND

21 y/o guit___

O___

Pr___
ab___
ho___

CA___
C___

A___
he___
ti___
d___
s___
cy___
pi___
be___
w___

AU___

Au___
ing___
will___
v'ee___
g___

PIER OF ___
NEW

PIER OF DEST___
USHUA___

GL___
NA___

*****

All we Need

ENTERTAINING
SEAS

DATE
06DEC2009

NAME OF PASSENGER
GLORIA FLEMING

PIER OF ORIGIN
NEW YORK, NY - U.S.A.
PIER OF DESTINATION
USHUAIA, ARGENTINA

_____

* * * * * * *

* *

AU
Au
ing
will
v'e

OKING

IT IS UNLAWFUL TO PURCHASE OR RESELL THIS TICKET FROM/TO ANY ENTITY OTHER THAN ISSUING CARRIER

is the
slightest
kiss of
the wind...

FRANCISCO

malbec syrah

de
MENDOZA
ARGENTINA

Made in General Alvear

ACKNOWLEDGMENTS

I would like to thank my partner, Rodrigo Corral, for his breathtaking talent and relentless energy, and without whom this story would be little more than a manual of instructions. A great deal of thanks also goes to Ben Schrank, a true visionary at Razorbill, for the idea in the first place, and for the many hours he served as our guide through this uncharted world; Jocelyn Davies, for her clear-headed insights and unwavering enthusiasm; and of course Jim Rutman, for giving me the opportunity to tell a story in a completely new way. —JESSICA

I would like to thank the brilliant Jessica Anthony for creating special characters in Glory and Frank; my favorite publisher Ben Schrank for his patience and support. Thank you, Doctor. Thanks to Frederick Schmitt, the team at Razorbill (Jocelyn Davies and Vivian Kirklin) and Jennifer Carrow for tying up loose ends. I would also like to thank Steve Attardo for his tireless effort in organizing, concepting, and designing *Chopsticks* with me (this book would not be as special without you). —RODRIGO

CREDITS

Glory: Rachel Fox
Frank: Ben Getz
Victor: Marc Scrivo
Maria: Jamie Neumann

Creative Direction: Rodrigo Corral Studio
Design: Steve Attardo, Elena Giavaldi and Devon Washburn
Photographers: Samantha Casolari and Frederick Schmitt
Additional photography: Susan Anthony
Retoucher: Even Yoo
Artwork: Matthew Buck
Producer: Liliana Bonafini